Ali's Bees

Bruce Olav Solheim

Illustrated by

Gabby Untermayerova

ISBN: 1544013981
ISBN-13: 978-1544013985
Library of Congress Control Number: 2017904125
CreateSpace Independent Publishing Platform, North Charleston, SC

DEDICATION

This book is dedicated to my grandson, Liam Stasko Solheim, born on November 23, 2016. May you possess the courage of a warrior, the mind of a scholar, the heart of a humanitarian, the imagination of an artist, and the soul of a poet.

CONTENTS

ACKNOWLEDGMENTS

I wish to thank Professor José Cruz González of California State University, Los Angeles, for his mentoring in shaping this story for the theater. I also wish to thank my actor friends at Citrus College who read the play and helped me bring the characters to life. I would also like to thank my wife, Ginger, Mary, Courtney, and the rest of my family, who supported me and encouraged me as this story took on its different forms. Special thanks to Gabby for her brilliant illustrations and to my editors, Erica, Devon, Laura, and Rachel.

GRANDFATHER

"I NOTICE little things," said Ali as his grandfather lovingly attended to his garden, accompanied by the buzzing of bees from his beehives.

"Like what, Ali?" asked his grandfather.

"Dust specks in the sunlight coming through our windows in the morning, clovers in our backyard, grains of sand at Sunset Beach, ants on the sidewalk," Ali continued.

"And bees?"

"Yes, *Jady*, I notice bees," said Ali, using the Arabic word for "grandfather" and smiling. He loved his grandfather and their cozy little home in the City of Angels—Los Angeles. His grandfather, Mohammad Salam, was in his seventies, wore a mixture of traditional Arab and Western clothing, and walked with a cane much of the time.

"Bees are unique among God's creatures. They improve our world, give us food, and do not prey on any other animal," explained Mr. Salam.

Ali looked at the bees buzzing around his grandfather and smiled. "I like that," he said. Ali began practicing throwing a baseball into his glove repeatedly.

"*Apis mellifera syriaca*, the honeybee indigenous to Iraq," Ali's grandfather said in a scholarly tone. "Our bees in Baquba were gentle, not aggressive."

As Ali listened, he thought about how his life had changed. He was an awkward but good-looking thirteen-year-old middle-school student who had seen more than his share of tragedy.

The late-afternoon sun cast long shadows that stretched to meet the faded, dusty yellow block wall in Mr. Salam's backyard. It was summertime, and the fresh green smell of the garden with flowers, vegetables, herbs, and the fragrance of the orange, lemon, and lime blossoms mingled with exhaust from the nearby freeway.

Ali put his head down, kicked some dirt, and threw his ball so hard into his glove that dust rose into the air.

Mr. Salam noticed and knowingly patted the boy's shoulder.

"*Jady, limatha alnnas eudwanioun la-haza al-darajeh?*" asked Ali in Arabic.

"Remember to speak English, Ali. We are in America," said his grandfather.

Ali shrugged his shoulders and repeated his question in English. "Why are people so aggressive, Grandfather?"

Mr. Salam glanced at Ali and continued to work in his garden as a truck horn sounded, reminding them both of the metropolis that surrounded their sanctu-

3

ary.

"They are not happy," answered the old man. He gave the boy an all-knowing, grandfatherly look.

The bees buzzed around Mr. Salam's head as he carefully watered his garden. Ali watched him for a while before he asked, "Why did you start working with bees, Jady?"

"Bees are mentioned in the Koran," said Mr. Salam proudly. "Beekeeping is a noble profession. I was a merchant for many years, but the nectar of the bees saved your grandmother when she was sick. After that, I became a beekeeper so I could honor and care for them."

Ali thought about this. He slowly moved over to an old, rusty garden chair and plopped down with a squeaky thud. He threw his glove to the ground, and the ball rolled under some bushes. He sat with his hands under his chin.

"What is it, Ali?" asked Mr. Salam.

"I miss Grandmother," said Ali softly.

"As do I," replied his grandfather, looking up wistfully toward the setting sun.

Ali stood up, grabbed a stick, and swished it

around, trying in vain to overcome a sudden rush of emotion.

"And my mother and father." Ali dropped the stick and wept gently.

Mr. Salam put his hand on his shoulder and patted him on the back.

Ali brought a dog-eared photo out of his pocket and looked at it closely. "Mother and Father," he repeated in a whisper.

Mr. Salam took the photo, smiled, and returned it to Ali, who tucked it back in his pocket.

"They wait for us. Families are forever, Ali," Mr. Salam said calmly.

Ali felt comforted and followed his grandfather to the hive. A bee landed on his hand, surprising him, and he shook it off violently.

"Gentle, Ali. They will not sting," advised Mr. Salam.

"How often do you get stung?" asked Ali.

Ali's grandfather picked up his smoker from the creaky old gardening table and patiently puffed smoke on the hive to calm the bees. "Not often. They will not sting you if you do not—what do you say?—freak out."

Ali looked at his grandfather, but he couldn't contain himself; he broke out into a wide grin, followed by an eruption of laughter. Surprised, his grandfather joined in. The shadows grew as the sun set on their city garden.

"You must make friends with the bees," added Mr. Salam. "If you feel comfortable, they feel comfortable, and they do not sting you."

"Yes, that makes sense," Ali acknowledged as his grandfather smiled and adjusted his glasses.

"Tell me about our home. I love your stories, Grandfather," said Ali.

Mr. Salam motioned for Ali to sit down as he put away his smoker and sat down next to him.

"Our honey in Baquba was the best," Mr. Salam explained proudly. "We planted orange trees among the date palms along the Diyala River. The date palms protected the oranges from the heat, and the palm sap dripped down onto the orange trees, making our oranges delicious. In the spring, the sweet fragrance of the trees was like perfume dancing in the air."

Ali closed his eyes and breathed in deeply through

his nose, imagining the sights and smells and ignoring the sounds of the city all around them. "I can see it and smell it, Jady," he whispered.

"Yes," said Mr. Salam.

Ali opened his eyes. "But the war?"

Mr. Salam stood up and shook his head as he remembered. "Yes, the war," he answered. "Saddam was a bad man, very bad. But when he was in power, I could travel the roads at night; I could move my bees around to help pollinate the orchards. After the invasion, Saddam was gone, but it was not safe to travel with so many insurgents. The checkpoints slowed me down, and the bees died. Many beekeepers were gone…and with them the bees." He sat back down and looked as if he saw something far away.

Ali softly touched his grandfather's weathered old hand. "Thank you, Grandfather. This will help me with my project."

"What project?"

"A science project in school," said Ali.

Mr. Salam smiled as he grabbed his cane that was by the chair and tapped it on the ground. "Ah, you will do well. You have always been a clever boy, Ali."

He rose from his chair, and they watched the bees for a while as a siren wailed in the distance.

Sirens frightened Ali. They reminded him of war and people being hurt. "I remember when I was little, I thought we all lived in the stomach of a giant," he said.

"Yes." Ali's grandfather listened as the bees continued their work all around them.

"And I thought there had to be people living inside of me too," said Ali with a smile.

Mr. Salam laughed quietly.

"And the giant was inside the stomach of a bigger giant, and so on," continued Ali.

"Imagination. Infinitely small and infinitely large," whispered Mr. Salam.

Ali became animated. "I would lie on the ground by the orange trees and look at the clouds and wonder if someone inside of my stomach was doing the same thing."

Mr. Salam looked over the top of his glasses at him. "It is important to sense the wonder of creation."

Ali took a moment to think about the loss of his

grandmother and parents in the war. He also feared losing his grandfather, the only family he had left. He stood up and walked a few measured steps before he turned around to speak. "I do not look at the clouds anymore, Grandfather. They just pass over my head silently."

Mr. Salam paused and gave Ali an empathetic look. He winced in pain as he stood up with the help of his cane. He walked over to Ali and touched his cheek tenderly with his leathery hand as a tear ran down Ali's face.

"What is troubling you, Ali?" asked Mr. Salam.

Ali was hesitant. He began to talk but stopped

and looked down as he wiped away his tears. "Sometimes I have these thoughts; I see things, hear things. I freeze up. Other kids notice."

"You have experienced war. It is normal," Mr. Salam explained as he again touched Ali gently on his cheek.

"I miss our home," said Ali quietly.

"Yes, but now this is our home. America," Ali's grandfather assured him.

Ali paused, looked up, and smiled as he thought about how peaceful their life was in America compared to war-torn Iraq.

"And you have your bees, Jady," said Ali.

Mr. Salam laughed. "Yes, I have my bees, and we have each other. We are lucky. *Alhamdulillah*." He hugged Ali, and they breathed in the wonderful mixture of fragrances from their garden refuge.

The sun set rapidly, and the bees, busily completing their day's work, buzzed all around them, the sound eventually giving way to the mechanical hum of the city.

2

SAVE THE BEES

THE NEXT day, Ali woke up early. He couldn't stop thinking about his bee project. He prepared breakfast for himself and his grandfather—hard-boiled eggs and wheat toast with butter; blackberry jam; and, of course, honey.

Ali watched the rolling bubbles in the boiling pot and noticed how the moist warmness fogged up their kitchen window. He drew a frowning face on the steamy window glass. After looking at it for a few seconds, he changed his mind, wiped it clear, and drew a smiling face.

Ali knew how long to cook the eggs so the delicious dark-orange yolk was not too firm and not too runny. The smell of toast filled the air.

Mr. Salam made coffee for himself, and then generously buttered his toast and drizzled his homemade golden honey on top.

The smell of blackberry jam and honey made Ali think of warm summer days. His grandfather's honey smelled and tasted like oranges, limes, lemons, clover, and grapes, with a hint of roses.

"Why are you in such a hurry, Ali?" asked Mr. Salam.

"Today we give our proposals for the science fair." Ali was almost breathless.

"I will clean up the breakfast dishes. You go ahead. Have fun," said Mr. Salam with a smile.

The boy hugged his grandfather and rushed out the door. Ali looked forward to talking to his class about the bee project.

"Well, goodbye, Ali," said Mr. Salam, laughing at the boy's frenzied hurry.

"Oh, goodbye, Grandfather," Ali called over his shoulder as he ran across their front yard, almost tripping on a garden gnome that Mr. Salam had received from Mrs. Washburn as a gift for helping to pollinate her roses.

Ali ran until he realized he had lots of time; then he slowed down and began to walk. There would be plenty of time to organize and plan once he arrived at school.

On his walk to school, Ali thought about his life in America. Sometimes life didn't seem to be fair. Some people had tremendous wealth and could have anything they wanted, while others remained sad and poor and went to bed hungry every night.

Ali noticed that in America, a country both he and his grandfather loved, that there were only a few wealthy people, and many poor. His grandfather told Ali that anyone could succeed in America if he or she worked hard enough, dreamed boldly, learned as much as possible, and had a little luck. It was the best country in the world, he often said.

Ali's grandfather loved Iraq, but the country of his birth had been at war for too long. Iraq provided no safety and little opportunity for Ali. Mr. Salam knew that moving to the United States would benefit his grandson in the long run.

Ali and his grandfather didn't live in an affluent part of town. The people who lived nearby were hardworking but not prosperous.

Mr. Mood worked at the convenience store, and

his wife had turned their home into a day care for several young children.

The Turners were both too sick to work, and, although they were kind to Ali on the rare occasions he saw them, their curtains were always closed. Mr. Salam said if they continued to live in the dark, they would never get well.

The Madrigal family had seven kids, and all of them played outside in their postage-stamp-sized yard and made a lot of noise.

Mrs. Washburn, a retired schoolteacher who fancied Ali's grandfather, had a prizewinning rose garden.

Despite their lack of wealth, the neighbors kept up their modest homes as best they could. They were friendly with Ali, and all of them loved his well-known grandfather—a neighborhood celebrity.

Ali attended a school several blocks from their home. He walked every morning and enjoyed the sights along the way. Ali knew all the neighborhood dogs—barkers and nonbarkers, biters and nonbiters. He waved to the cats in the windows that stared at him as he passed, and he pet the ones that came up to

him and flopped down on the sidewalk at his feet, like
the tubby tabby cat named Señor.

He arrived early at school that day and prepared
his speech. His classroom was rather shabby; the ceil-
ing tiles were water-soaked, and some were in the
process of collapse. The desks and chairs were worn-
out and in need of repair. Some of the school build-
ings had graffiti on them, but Ali didn't know what
the letters spelled.

Ali's teacher, Ms. Waters, was a sweet lady who
had gone out of her way to make Ali comfortable
when he came from Iraq. She always wore cardigan
sweaters and smelled like lilacs.

Ali patiently waited as a few other kids gave their
science-project proposals. Finally, it was his turn. Ms.
Waters smiled at him as he walked up to the front of

the class and cleared his throat before he spoke. Ali often lacked confidence, but he believed in his project. His belief gave him strength.

"Last year I began to notice honeybees that were dead or dying. Wherever I went, I saw them, their little bodies struggling on the ground, I felt sorry for them. They are hard workers, like my parents were, and my grandfather—he was a beekeeper in Iraq. We lived in Baquba, north of Baghdad, surrounded by orange trees. I want to find out what is killing the honeybees. My science project will look at the importance of bees and how we can save them," Ali said confidently.

He breathed a sigh of relief after he finished. A few kids applauded along with Ms. Waters. Lupe, a tall, slender, cute girl, ran up and hugged Ali. He blushed.

"I want to help. Can we work together on this project for the science fair?" Lupe asked enthusiastically.

Ms. Waters looked at both of them as Lupe smiled broadly. "Yes, you can have partners on your projects," said Ms. Waters.

"*¡Excelente!*" yelled Lupe.

Ali made his way back to his seat and sat in silence for a few moments. Intrusive memories of the war often weighed heavily on his mind.

Lupe noticed and looked disappointed. "Ali, can we work together? I mean…if it's OK with you?" she asked.

Ali finally acknowledged her with a smile. "Sure, that would be very good," he said.

Lupe smiled widely and giggled. She observed Ali more carefully. "You OK?" she asked.

"Yes. Sometimes I am thinking loudly in my head," he said.

"That's OK. I'm so excited!" said Lupe exuberantly.

Another boy, named Jenks, sat near Ali. He couldn't be described as a happy boy, and he had a reputation of being a bully. "If you ask me, it's stupid," he said with a sour look on his face.

"Didn't ask, and, by the way, it's an important project, Señor Grumpy," Lupe said.

Ali looked at Jenks.

"Maybe you want to work together with us?" he asked.

Jenks looked at both Lupe and Ali and down at the floor.

"Yeah, work with us," said Lupe.

Ms. Waters said, "You can have a maximum of three in your group."

Jenks looked down at the floor while Ms. Waters, Lupe, and Ali stared at him. The other kids in the classroom grew restless, while Jenks grew visibly frustrated.

"I'm not working with a terrorist!" he blurted out. He ran out of the classroom.

Stunned, nobody said anything. Finally, Ms. Waters broke the silence. "It's all right, students. Let's take a short break. I'll be right back." She sprang out of the door after Jenks.

Ali looked at Lupe in shock. "Why did he say that?" he asked.

"He's been angry since his dad came back from the war," responded Lupe calmly.

"Iraq?" asked Ali.

"Yeah."

Ali flashed back to the horrors he had seen in Iraq. He gazed upward and focused outside of the classroom window. "The war took away many things," he said solemnly.

Ali and Lupe stood in silence for a moment as the other kids got loud and out of control. This rambunctious behavior ended as soon as Ms. Waters returned.

"Work in your groups for a while, students," she said.

Ali and Lupe sat down next to each other.

"Ali, tell me more about honeybees," Lupe said.

"Honeybees are responsible for much of our food," said Ali.

Lupe opened her lunch bag and brought out her sandwich. "You mean like this ham sandwich?" she asked with a smile.

"No," said Ali, laughing. He peered into her lunch bag and grabbed her apple. "But bees helped make this apple."

Lupe jumped up and down and danced around. "We're going to win first place in the science fair. We're going to win first place in the science fair," she sang as she danced.

"I hope so," said Ali.

Finally, Lupe sat back down after Ms. Waters gave her one of her special looks.

"I'm an artist, you know," the girl said.

"Good," said Ali.

"I can draw, and I've got really neat handwriting."

"We will make a good team," said Ali.

Lupe smiled because she knew exactly what to do. "You know, Jenks is really smart and can build almost anything," she said.

Ali hung his head in silence. Then he whispered, "I think he hates me."

"Ah, he's not a bad guy," said Lupe.

"All right," said Ali as he wrote in his notebook.

"Once you get to know him, talk to him," she

added.

"Did you know honeybees communicate by smell and by dances?" asked Ali.

"Dances?"

"Yes. They get right next to each other and buzz and dance and wiggle their bottoms," he said.

Lupe's infectious giggling made him laugh too.

She stood up and grabbed Ali's hands. She pulled him up on his feet. She began to dance, bumping her hips against his while she made a buzzing sound. Ali blushed.

"Like this?" asked Lupe.

Ali joined in the dance, and they both giggled.

"Yes, that is it," said Ali with a grin.

Unbeknownst to Lupe and Ali, Jenks had returned and was watching them from the doorway. He had his hands in his pockets, and he kept watching Ali and Lupe having fun; he grew more and more jealous, until he looked down and kicked the door in frustration.

Finally, Ms. Waters cleared her throat. "All right, you two busy bees, time to sit down and work quietly."

The other students giggled. Jenks continued to stand in the doorway, looking at the ground and brooding; then he turned quickly and left.

3

TAKE ME OUT TO THE BALL GAME

THE NEXT afternoon, Jenks and his father, Mr. Hooper, were at the community baseball field by the dugout fence. Jenks was an athletic, handsome, multi-racial boy who looked very much like his father. The field was in poor condition, with large washed-out ruts, uncut grass, trash, and rusty chain-link fencing.

Jenks threw a baseball into his glove repeatedly, waiting for the right moment to speak to his father. Mr. Hooper was a ruggedly good-looking man in his late thirties. He had a careworn face and had his old army medical bag slung over his shoulder. He sat in his wheelchair, with one hand on the fence, staring off toward the horizon.

Jenks tried desperately to get his father's attention. "I'll hit a homer for ya today, Dad," he said.

Mr. Hooper continued to stare toward the horizon. Many combat veterans did the same because of the trauma of war. Psychologists and veterans called this the thousand-yard stare.

"Got a B on my math test," Jenks added, but his dad didn't acknowledge him.

Ali quietly sat down in the dugout and watched them, unbeknownst to Jenks and his father.

"Dickie went camping with his dad. They went fishing. Caught eight really big trout!" said Jenks as he indicated the imagined length.

Finally, Mr. Hooper looked at his son with sad eyes. "Good for them," he said gruffly.

Jenks looked down at the ground, frustrated. "Dad, maybe you should call Mom. Ya know, maybe she'll wanna come over for dinner," he said.

Mr. Hooper's expression changed from sadness to anger in a heartbeat. "Don't start that with me. No, not gonna happen!" he yelled.

Ali felt sorry for Jenks. He could see that Jenks was trying to get Mr. Hooper's attention. "Dad, wanna play catch?" Jenks asked as he handed his father the baseball.

Mr. Hooper looked at the ball closely. He closed his eyes and gripped it tightly. After a few moments, Mr. Hooper opened his eyes and stared into the distance. Ali could see that he was shaking slightly.

A distant siren wailed, and Jenks, distracted, looked away. Ali kept his focus on Mr. Hooper who, like Ali, also seemed to be frozen in thought by the siren. Ali's mind raced with horrific images of war. After the siren had faded, Mr. Hooper threw the baseball to Jenks, accidentally hitting him in the stomach and frightening him.

Jenks fell to the ground as the ball rolled away. Ali noticed that Jenks tried hard not to cry.

Mr. Hooper looked embarrassed, but this quickly turned to anger. "What did I teach you? Pay attention! Keep your head down! That's what war is like, but all the time. McGraw didn't listen, got it right between the eyes in Fallujah!"

Jenks picked himself up, struggling not to cry.

"Don't you dare cry!" yelled Mr. Hooper.

Jenks looked sad and angry at the same time.

"Yes, Father," he muttered.

Mr. Hooper began to roll away.

"Aren't you staying for the game?" asked Jenks.

Annoyed, Mr. Hooper stopped and turned his wheelchair around. "No. Just head over to the Cozy Inn after. I'll be there." He turned back around and rolled away.

Jenks picked up the baseball that had hit him and threw it into his glove again, harder and harder. Ali popped up from the bench and approached Jenks.

"What are you doing here?" asked Jenks angrily. He continued to pound the ball into his glove.

"Came to play the baseball," answered Ali cheerfully.

"Not *the* baseball. Just say 'baseball,'" said Jenks.

He grew more impatient and angry.

"What?" said Ali.

Jenks positioned himself in front of Ali. "Give it up. You're hopeless," he said.

Ali picked up a bat and swung it awkwardly. "I know, but my grandfather tells me I have to try." He put down the bat and practiced an awkward throwing motion.

Jenks pointed aggressively at Ali. "Why don't you just go back to where ya came from?"

"I cannot," responded Ali wistfully.

Jenks grew even more impatient. "Why not?"

"This is our home," said Ali.

"Well, that sucks," said Jenks with a mean smile. He circled Ali as his taunting intensified. "Your grandfather Taliban too?" he asked.

The question hurt Ali. "No, he is a good man. Shiite Muslim," he said defiantly.

Jenks did not understand.

"Taliban are in Afghanistan. We are from Iraq," said Ali to clarify.

Jenks continued to circle Ali relentlessly. "What's the difference? You're all terrorists, right?" Ali did not respond to his taunting.

Instead, Ali thought quietly about what had happened to him, his grandfather, his grandmother, and his parents.

The silence proved to be too much for Jenks. "You're strange," he said in an attempt to break the awkward silence.

"Why do you say this?" asked Ali, snapping out of his deep thoughts.

"You stare and say nothing," Jenks said.

"Sometimes I have to think."

"Yeah, well, think around someone else. It's creepy," Jenks said, trying to keep the upper hand.

"My grandfather says he sees your father at the Cozy Inn," said Ali.

"How does he know?" Jenks snapped. The comment caught him off guard.

"Grandfather watches the games there," said Ali with a smile.

"So what? Who cares?" Jenks tried to regain control of the conversation.

"He says your father is an angry man," Ali said with concern.

Jenks stopped in his tracks. His frustration and anger were building in defense of his father. "Mind your own business!" he yelled. He threw his baseball at Ali.

The ball struck Ali on the arm. He fell to the ground, startled.

"Guess you don't know how to duck either," said Jenks, thoroughly satisfied with himself.

Ali stood up and rubbed his sore arm. "Why did you do that?" he asked.

Jenks noticed that Ali didn't cry. This seemed to make him even more upset. "Oh, you're really gonna get it now," he said as he charged at Ali.

Then Lupe arrived and grabbed Jenks by the arm.

"*Hola*," she said cheerfully. "What are you guys doing?"

Jenks got quiet. "Hi," he said meekly. He walked away, staring at Ali.

Lupe sensed something. "What happened?" she asked Ali.

"I forgot to duck."

"No. What happened with Jenks?" Lupe was trying to figure out the situation.

Ali rubbed his arm. "I asked about his father," he said.

"Oh," said Lupe.

"Why is his father in a wheelchair?" asked Ali innocently. He and Lupe slowly walked over to the dugout.

"He fought in Iraq," answered Lupe. They stood in silence for a moment. "He was wounded," she added.

Now Ali understood. "I never see his mother at the games," he said as he and Lupe sat in the dugout.

"She left. Like my mama says, 'Living separately, *mija*,'" explained Lupe, imitating her mother.

Ali smiled. "Why does his father carry a bag?"

Lupe playfully grabbed the baseball from Ali.

"It's a military medical bag. He worked as a medic in the army," she explained.

Ali tried to get the ball back from Lupe, but she hid it from him.

"My father was a policeman," said Ali with pride.

"Really? Cool," said Lupe.

"My mother was a seamstress. Made all our clothes," Ali added.

Lupe chose her words carefully. "Your parents…where are they?" She handed the ball back.

Ali hesitated. He heard loud voices. "Jenks is coming back!" he said.

"It's OK. Let me—" Lupe said, but Ali moved so frantically that she couldn't finish.

"I have to go. Bye," he said. He ran toward home, leaving Lupe sitting on the bench, perplexed.

Jenks and his friends arrived in a cloud of dust. Jenks looked all around for Ali but saw only Lupe smiling and sitting in the dugout.

4

THE GREAT AND POWERFUL

ALI HELPED his grandfather in the garden later that day. The sun sank low on the horizon, and traffic noises were intensifying as people rushed to get home for dinner. Mr. Salam hummed an old song as he trimmed some bushes with clippers, while the boy gathered the cuttings and put them in a bucket.

"You know, if a bee is sick, she does not return to the hive," said Mr. Salam.

"Why, Grandfather?" asked Ali.

"She flies off and dies alone so that she does not infect the rest of the colony," said Mr. Salam with smiling eyes.

Ali thought more about the answer. "That is sad."

The old man stopped trimming for a moment and

turned to Ali, using his finger to accentuate his words. "Sometimes the one must sacrifice for the many," Mr. Salam said.

Ali smiled and continued to pick up the trimmings. "I learned that bees work hard and help each other. They only live for thirty days because they work themselves to death," he said proudly, knowing that his grandfather would appreciate how much he had studied.

Mr. Salam smiled broadly. "Yes, no such thing as a lazy bee."

"Yes, Jady," said the boy.

They both laughed. They continued their trimming as Ali thought deeply.

"You said bees are mentioned in the Koran?" asked Ali.

Mr. Salam smiled and began to speak as he trimmed. "It is said, 'And of the fruits of the palms and the grapes, you obtain from them goodly provision. And the Lord revealed to the bee: make hives in the mountains and in the trees and in what they build. Then eat of all the fruits and walk in the ways of the Lord submissively. There comes forth from their bellies a beverage of many hues, in which there is healing for men. Allah the knowing, powerful, the merciful, the beneficent,'" said Mr. Salam triumphantly.

The boy smiled at his grandfather.

"The Koran is the only holy book that mentions bees," Mr. Salam added.

Bang! A junky car cruising their street backfired, startling Ali.

"What is it, Ali?" Mr. Salam noticed the boy's worried look and sensed his sadness.

"I am having those bad dreams," answered Ali.

"Nightmares," said Mr. Salam, almost under his breath.

"Terrible storms. The clouds turn black," Ali said. He sounded frightened.

"Yes." Mr. Salam paid close attention to Ali.

"Loud explosions, all around. Fire so bright that I cannot look away, even though I want to," continued Ali, his eyes wide.

"Frightening," said Mr. Salam.

"Yes, I wake up with my heart beating so fast." Ali held his chest.

"I have noticed you do not sleep well," said Mr.

Salam. He patted Ali on the shoulder.

"I am afraid to go to sleep," said Ali, trying to hold back his emotions.

Mr. Salam put down his clippers and sat in one of the rusty lawn chairs.

Ali sat down next to his grandfather, placing his bucket between them. "I remember being all alone in the camp, with the other orphans, before I found you," said Ali, staring off into the distance as he spoke. "There was no safe place for us to sleep and not enough food."

"This is normal. You and I have seen war firsthand, Ali. The nightmares try to steal the courage we build up during the daytime," said Mr. Salam reassuringly.

"Yes, Jady," Ali said with a worried smile.

"So we must start all over again the next day," added Mr. Salam.

"The fear freezes me," Ali said.

"Even the bravest person is still afraid. Bravery is not the absence of fear. It is working through the fear, day by day," said Ali's grandfather, smiling.

"Does it get better?" asked Ali.

Mr. Salam wiped his spectacles clean with a cloth and put them in his pocket. "If you mean does it go away, no. But you can become familiar with the source of your fear and draw strength from your experiences." He attempted to grab his clippers but fell back into his chair, holding his sore back. He raised himself again slowly from the old, rusty lawn chair.

Ali grabbed the clippers and handed them to his grandfather to help him.

"We have to carry on, stay busy, like our honey-bees. There is comfort in routines, a sense of predict-ability and safety," said Mr. Salam.

The boy hugged his grandfather as a horn sound-ed, followed by a bass-heavy car stereo that triggered a few car alarms. His grandfather started trimming once again.

Ali stood silent for a while, listening to the city noises in their garden oasis. A few bees buzzed by his head, but he remained calm as his grandfather had instructed him.

"Another boy threatened me," he said.

Mr. Salam peeked at Ali before continuing with his work. "What did you do?"

"I ran away," said Ali sheepishly.

"I see," said Mr. Salam.

Ali kicked some dirt and looked down as he thought about the incident. "Does that mean I am a coward?"

Mr. Salam stopped trimming and smiled. "You are a victim of disorganized thinking. You are under the unfortunate impression that just because you ran away, you have no courage; you are confusing courage with wisdom." Ali's grandfather's eyes were all-knowing.

"Wisdom?" asked the boy.

"Yes." Mr. Salam was steadfast.

"Is that from the Koran?"

Mr. Salam peered over his glasses at Ali again.

"No, *The Wizard of Oz*," he answered with a playful smile.

Ali stared at his grandfather in amazement.

"Great American wisdom from Hollywood," added Mr. Salam. They both grinned.

Ali and his grandfather continued their work under a spectacular sunset as the bees buzzed around their heads and finished their own jobs for the evening.

THE WAR AT HOME

ON A WARM, sunny afternoon a few days later, Ali and Jenks stood next to each other on the sadly neglected community baseball field. Jenks slammed his fist rhythmically into his baseball glove, and Ali awkwardly tried to do the same.

"You struck out with the bases loaded. Again," said Jenks angrily.

"I tried. I have trouble hitting the ball when it is thrown so fast," Ali said.

Jenks squared himself in front of Ali, ready, as always, for confrontation.

"C'mon, that kid threw so slow even a girl coulda hit it," Jenks taunted.

"I have seen girls hit. They are very good." Ali's tone was earnest.

Jenks grew frustrated. "Never mind. You've got

no business being on our team," he snapped. He surveyed the field for witnesses, and then pushed Ali, who barely managed to stay on his feet.

"You can't run, you can't catch, you can't throw, and you can't hit," said Jenks.

"I know," said Ali sheepishly.

Jenks's frustration grew to new heights. "You know? I just dissed you. That don't make you mad?"

"No. It is true—I am a terrible player, but I do my best," said Ali earnestly.

"Nobody wants you on the team." Jenks was relentless.

"Really? Was there a vote?" asked Ali.

"No! Everybody thinks you stink."

"My odor offends?" Ali was turning out to be quite an impressive verbal sparring partner for Jenks.

"No, you stink at playing baseball!" yelled Jenks, losing his composure.

Ali didn't respond, so Jenks pushed him, this time a bit harder. Ali stood his ground and didn't fall.

"Why don't you fight back?" asked Jenks, now exasperated.

"I do not want to fight," Ali said.

A stray dog began barking loudly, which served to increase the tension between the boys.

"Forget it. Ain't happening," said Jenks defiantly.

"My grandfather said that—"

Jenks cut him off. "Grandfather? Where's your mom and dad?"

Ali remained silent and tried hard not to rekindle his painful memories.

"What kind of weirdo lives with their grandfather anyway?" asked Jenks, persisting in his taunting of Ali.

"I am not sure what you mean," Ali said as a siren

wailed and warbled several blocks away, causing all the neighborhood dogs to howl.

"Who cares about your grandfather? He's a terrorist too, I'm sure," Jenks said.

An ice-cream vendor walked slowly past the boys, jingling his bell.

Ali thought carefully about what to say. "I told you he is a good and kind man."

"Whatever," said Jenks. He dropped his glove and threw his hands up in the air.

"Male bees do not have fathers, only grandfathers," added Ali.

Jenks pointed at Ali. "What? You're lying."

"It is true."

"The other guys think you should go back to wherever you came from," Jenks said as the stray dog on the ball field once again began barking loudly at invisible enemies.

"I cannot go back. I told you."

Jenks picked up his glove again and slammed his fist into the pocket several times. Dust rose from the well-seasoned leather.

"My dad said your people took down the Twin

Towers on 9/11," said Jenks with an unfriendly smile.

"The 9/11 terrorists were from Saudi Arabia, Egypt, Lebanon, and the United Arab Emirates. Not Iraq," Ali explained defiantly.

Jenks circled Ali again as a car rolled by, playing loud rap music. "We had to invade Afghanistan and Iraq to get those terrorists," he said.

"Iraq had nothing to do with 9/11." Ali was emphatic.

Jenks smiled and examined the laces on his baseball glove. "Sure, that's what they all say," he said. Breaking the relative calm of the moment, he pushed Ali violently to the ground and then stood above the stunned boy in a threatening posture.

"Don't just lie there. Aren't you scared?" asked Jenks.

"I am afraid, but I cannot run," said Ali. His voice quivered.

"Go before I punch you for real, OK?" Jenks said as he kicked the dirt. "Why do you want to hurt me?" asked Ali as his courage built up again.

"Don't confuse me. You know why," responded Jenks, looking dejected.

"No, I do not know why," Ali said. Jenks shifted his weight from one leg to the other; Ali could see that the boy felt uncomfortable.

"Well, for one thing, leave Lupe alone. She's my girl," Jenks said.

"Lupe?"

"Yeah, Lupe." Jenks's face had flushed a bit.

"Your girl? I do not understand," said Ali.

"What are ya, stupid or something?"

"I do not think so," Ali said innocently.

"You better not think she's your girlfriend," said Jenks, his anger peaking again.

Ali finally understood and smiled. "Oh, I see. She is my friend, but—" Ali started to explain just before Jenks again pushed him hard to the ground. Jenks stood over him with a clenched fist.

Then Lupe arrived at a run. She grabbed Jenks. "Stop it! *Ai, que* mean!" she yelled. She helped Ali get back on his feet and dusted him off.

Jenks stood nearby with his hands in his pockets and his head down as Lupe stared at him sternly.

"It is all right. I am fine," said Ali.

"It's not fine. This has to stop!" Lupe insisted.

Jenks and Ali stared at her, not knowing what to do or say next.

"I want us all to work together on the science project," she insisted.

"No way," said Jenks.

Lupe focused on him intently. "Listen, Ali is really smart—"

Jenks interrupted her. "I don't care," he blurted.

"You be nice, *tipo duro*," said Lupe, calling Jenks a tough guy. "He's my friend."

Jenks kicked the dirt again in frustration. "All right."

Lupe smiled. "I have to go and get some Tylenol for my mama. Her boyfriend broke up with her last night. *Muy dramatica*."

This piqued Ali's curiosity. "Boyfriend? Where is your father?" he asked.

Lupe thought for a moment as Jenks gave Ali a dirty look. "Juárez, I think. He doesn't live with us anymore," she said.

"Is that in Mexico?" asked Ali.

"Yeah, he was deported by *la migra*, US immigration," she said.

"Was he illegal?" asked Jenks.

"No, just not documented," said Lupe, matter-of-factly hiding her deep worries.

"I am sorry," said Ali with sympathy.

"He's a *campesino*, a farm worker. He works very hard. Mama too. She has two jobs: cleans houses, then waitresses at night. I take care of my brother and sister and my cousin…and my mom when she gets sad," Lupe said.

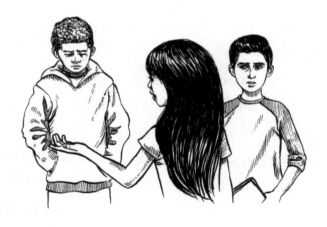

"Is she sad very often?" asked Ali.

Jenks continued to look at him with contempt.

"Yeah, a lot lately. Money problems, so I help with babysitting for neighbors," Lupe said. They were all silent for a moment.

"The queen bee," Ali blurted out. He smiled.

"That's me," said Lupe. She smiled back, and then turned to go. "See you both later, OK?"

Jenks and Ali both nodded. The girl skipped away, humming a tune.

Jenks fixed his anger again on Ali, poking him in the chest, much to Ali's surprise.

"This ain't over by a long shot," Jenks warned. He turned and walked across the outfield. What was Jenks going to do? What could Ali do to resolve the conflict? These were just some of the thoughts Ali had as he stood alone on the baseball field.

The ice-cream vendor walked by again, pushing his cart with the jingling bell.

FRIENDS

AFTER THE school bell finished ringing, Ali and Lupe quickly sat down at their well-worn desks. It was project-work day. Ms. Waters had written instructions for the science-project groups on the board. While Lupe opened her binder to find a pen, Ali focused on a baseball card he was holding in both hands.

"What's that?" asked Lupe.

"A baseball card." Ali beamed and handed the card to Lupe, who examined it carefully.

"Mickey Mantle. I think that's an old card," Lupe said and gave the card back to Ali.

"Yes, my grandfather gave it to me," Ali said proudly as he tucked the card into his binder. Jenks walked in and, with a stern look from Ms. Waters, sat at his desk near Lupe and Ali.

Lupe opened her notebook and began writing. "OK, so we got to get started on this project," she said.

"What project?" asked Jenks.

Lupe rolled her eyes and glanced sharply at him. "For science. Our science project for the science fair."

Jenks glared at the notebook and Ali. "I'll do my own," he said.

"The teacher wants us to work in groups," said Ali.

Jenks pointed at him. "I don't wanna be in your group. Get it?"

Lupe laid her pen down on the notebook and spoke sternly. "We'll win the science fair if we work together," she said.

This did not move Jenks. Ali looked at Jenks, which made Jenks feel uncomfortable.

"What?" asked Jenks, growing annoyed.

Ali opened his binder and pulled out the Mickey Mantle baseball card.

"I want you to have this," he said. He handed the card carefully to Jenks, who examined it closely and with reverence.

"Hall of Famer Mickey Mantle," said Jenks with amazement.

"That is what they tell me," said Ali with pride.

"Are you sure you should give it away?" asked Lupe. Jenks and Lupe both glanced at Ali, looking for reassurance.

Ali opened his hands in a kind gesture to Jenks. "I want you to have it," he said earnestly.

Jenks admired the unique quality and value of the old card. "He was my dad's favorite player. He talks about him all the time," the boy said with a hint of sentiment. Ali and Jenks were both smiling.

Lupe enjoyed the moment but returned to her

project notebook. "Can we get to work now?"

"Sure," said Ali. He laid out some papers from his binder and studied them strategically.

The bright and happy look on Jenks's face soon turned to concern, confusion, and frustration. He placed the card on the desk and left the classroom abruptly as Ms. Waters looked over her shoulder to see what had happened.

"Jenks, where you going?" asked Lupe, too late.

"What happened?" asked Ali.

Lupe thought for a moment. "He's conflicted. He can't handle you being nice to him."

"Why?"

"Because he's not been nice to you."

"Oh. You sure are smart," said Ali, smiling.

"You're smart. I'm clever and wise," Lupe said.

Ali thought about this. "What is the difference?" he asked.

Lupe just smirked and kept writing.

Outside the classroom, Ms. Waters found Jenks upset, sitting with his hands on his head. With a caring and concerned look, she urged him to come back to class. Ms. Waters had a sixth sense. A kind and considerate teacher, she always knew what her students were thinking and feeling.

Jenks stood up slowly, and Ms. Waters gave him a reassuring smile. He came back and sat down quietly as Ms. Waters returned to her desk, and the rest of the class again focused on their projects. Jenks cautiously picked up the Mickey Mantle card and tried to hand it to Ali.

"No, I want you to have it," Ali said.

Jenks could not hold his head high as he usually did. "I can't," he said sheepishly.

"Why?" asked Ali.

Lupe winked at Ali and smiled as she glanced at Jenks. "Do you feel guilty, *tipo duro*? Huh?" she asked.

"What? I dunno. No!" said Jenks, slightly embarrassed.

Lupe hugged Jenks, which surprised him. "There's hope for you yet, like my mama says," she said.

"I just want to be your friend," said Ali.

Jenks thought deeply for a moment. "I know, I know. This card…it'll mean a lot to my dad, but you don't know…" Jenks looked like he was fighting against his emotions coming to the surface.

"Maybe it will help?" asked Ali. He motioned for Jenks to keep the card.

"Thanks," Jenks said. He lifted his head up slightly to look at Ali. A moment of silence eventually gave way to the usual classroom noise as the students, temporarily distracted, returned to their group projects.

"See, all taken care of. Now can we get to work?" asked Lupe with a warm smile.

"Yeah." Ali was confident.

"I guess so," said Jenks reluctantly.

Lupe showed the two boys her plans. "OK, I've drawn this to show how the display should look." She pointed out different aspects of the drawing.

Jenks and Ali examined it with care.

"Jenks, you're good at building things, so you put together the frame and the hinges. See how it moves?" Lupe asked.

"Yeah, I can do that," said Jenks.

Lupe held his hand for a moment. "I know you can," she said.

Ali kept up his excitement. "I will give you all the

information about bees and set up the field study," he said.

"Great, and I'll do all the lettering and artwork," said Lupe. The boys were busy drawing and writing in their project notebooks.

Ms. Waters smiled when she saw Jenks working together peacefully with Lupe and Ali.

"Did you know bees can fly up to fifteen miles per hour?" asked Ali.

Jenks and Lupe continued to work and were politely listening at best.

"Bees are the only insect that makes food for humans," added Ali.

"Honey, right? I love honey," said Lupe as she kept drawing.

"And all the worker bees are female," continued Ali.

Lupe took notice of this particular bee fact. "Of course they are," she said. She and Ali laughed.

"Bees have been around for twenty million years—" said Ali before Jenks, growing frustrated, interrupted him.

"Bees, bees, bees. That's all you two talk about!"

he complained, loudly enough that Ms. Waters took off her glasses and stared at him. As the other students returned to their studies, Lupe and Ali continued to fix their eyes on Jenks.

"Hello? Working on our science project...*about bees*," Lupe said. She nudged Ali, urging him to continue with his astounding bee facts, while Jenks heaved a sigh.

"And besides honey, the bees make wax and royal jelly," said Ali.

Lupe and Jenks both looked at him.

"Royal jelly?" asked Jenks. He and Lupe looked at each other, and Lupe shrugged her shoulders.

"Royal jelly is a honeybee secretion used to feed the larvae in the colony. And when worker bees—"

Lupe interrupted him. "Who are all girls, right?"

Ali nodded. "Yes, all female. When they decide to make a new queen because the old one is either weak or dead, they choose special larvae and feed them with lots of royal jelly in specially built queen cells. The extra feeding makes the queen," said Ali with pride.

"The queen bee—that's me," Lupe said. Ali and

Lupe laughed, and Ms. Waters smiled at them.

Jenks, however, had become serious.

"Then, when the queen is fully developed, it is time for the courtship flight with the drones," said Ali.

This information piqued Jenks's interest. "Drones? Like what we attack the terrorists with?" he asked.

Other kids in the class giggled and were quickly silenced by Ms. Waters.

"No. Drones are the male bees," Ali said.

"And the queen chooses, right?" asked Lupe.

"Yeah," responded Ali.

They continued to work, and soon it became apparent that Jenks had a crush on Lupe. He stared longingly at her. His nervousness made him sweat, and his palms became wet and clammy. Lupe noticed the extra attention from Jenks, but Ali just continued to assemble bee facts.

Lupe caught Jenks staring a few times; each time, he looked away quickly, only to again become fixated on her. His perspiration dripped onto his desk and his report book. Jenks's obsession started to make Lupe uncomfortable.

"*¿Que?* Are you going to be sick?" she asked Jenks.

Beyond the point of no return, Jenks had to ask her something. "Lupe?" he asked nervously.

"Yeah?"

"Which one of us do you like better?" Jenks asked.

An awkward silence commenced as Ali looked up from his work.

A few other kids giggled, only to once again be silenced by Ms. Waters with a single glance.

"What?" asked Lupe, looking for clarification before she gave her response.

"You know, *like*-like?" Jenks's hands were trembling.

Lupe put her hands on her hips and tilted her head. "Do you think I'm just here for you to look at?" she asked in a cheeky way.

"No," said Jenks.

"Just a pretty face? Huh?"

"Yes, ah, no…" said Ali, confused.

"Do you think I'm some *chica* looking for a boyfriend?" Lupe asked with persistence.

"No, but—" answered a bewildered Jenks.

"I have a brain, for your information," Lupe said proudly.

"Yes," Ali agreed.

"I'm just as smart and strong as you," continued Lupe.

"Yes," Ali agreed again.

"Yeah," Jenks said.

Lupe paused, looked away, and looked back again at the overmatched boys.

"*And* I have a pretty face," she said. The boys looked at each other in amazement.

"Listen, *amigos*, I like both of you. You're both special to me. I'm not choosing one of you over the other. Just friends. Get it?"

"Yes," said Ali.

"OK," said Jenks.

"My mama has boyfriends, and from what I've seen, none of them treat her nice. So forget it. No boyfriends," asserted Lupe.

The boys both felt embarrassed as Ms. Waters smiled at all of them.

"Besides, don't the drones die after being chosen by the queen?" asked Lupe.

"Yes, that is true," answered Ali.

"Well, consider yourselves lucky, *niños*," said Lupe.

Ms. Waters could not help but laugh to herself, having overheard the conversation.

Ali, Lupe, and Jenks returned to their work as the day wore on and the clock ticked ever so slowly on the wall.

MICKEY MANTLE

WHEN ALI got home after school, he tried to hide his nervousness. He had to tell his grandfather about giving away the Mickey Mantle baseball card. He waited until the early evening to approach his grandfather.

Ali walked out into the garden, where his grandfather was checking the frames in his beehive and using his smoker to calm the bees. A magnificent multicolored sunset celebrated another busy day for both people and bees. The sounds of a passing car and dogs barking at perceived threats occasionally drowned out the constant buzzing of the bees.

Ali finally built up enough courage to talk to his grandfather. "I have something to tell you, Jady."

Mr. Salam continued working. "What is it, Ali?" he asked.

Ali paused. "I gave away that baseball card you gave me," he said quickly, hoping for the best.

"You did? The Mickey Mantle?" His grandfather's calm tone surprised Ali.

"I am sorry, Jady," said Ali.

Mr. Salam thought for a moment. "Part of the reason I gave you the card was to inspire you in baseball and life," he explained.

"I know," said Ali tentatively.

"Who did you give it to?" Mr. Salam asked.

"Jenks, the boy who threatened me," Ali said.

This surprised Mr. Salam. "I see. That is interesting."

Ali followed his grandfather as he checked more frames in the hive. "I understand if you are angry with me," he said sorrowfully.

Mr. Salam stopped working for a moment and drifted into memory. "That Mickey Mantle card was a gift from my friend Colonel Bill," he said.

"I should have asked you," Ali said apologetically.

"I am surprised, but I am not angry. Material things are transitory," said Mr. Salam as he examined his hive. "I gave it to you, so its meaning and value were transferred, and I have no say in its disposition. When you give, you should give with an open heart."

"Are you sure?" asked Ali.

"I worked as a translator for Colonel Bill in 2003 during the American invasion. We both loved baseball, and he knew I was a fan of the New York Yankees," continued Mr. Salam.

"Yankees?"

Mr. Salam smiled broadly. "Oh yes. Babe Ruth, Lou Gehrig, Joe DiMaggio, Derek Jeter…and my favorite, Mickey Mantle."

"I did not know how special it was," said Ali.

Mr. Salam placed his hand on the boy's shoulder. "Baseball is part of the reason I love America," he said. "It is truly American. That is why I wanted you to learn to play. Baseball teaches life lessons." Mr. Salam gave the smoker to Ali to hold while he closely examined some of the honeycomb.

"Really?" asked Ali.

"Did you know even the best hitters in baseball fail seven out of ten times at bat?" asked Mr. Salam.

Ali listened intently. He was amazed by his grandfather's kindness and wisdom. "I did not know that," he said.

"Every player has a special skill and job to do, just like our bees. They play the game until it is over, no matter how long it takes," explained Mr. Salam as he took the smoker back from Ali.

"I did not think of it that way," said Ali.

"And the goal is to get home, just like our bees returning to the hive, their home," Mr. Salam said, admiring his hives. "It is not over until it is over."

"That sounds like it is from the Koran, Jady."

"No, the great American philosopher Yogi Berra. Also a New York Yankee," said Mr. Salam with a wink.

Ali glanced at his grandfather and smiled. He followed him as he put away his smoker and sat in one of the two rusty lawn chairs.

"I gave that card to you so you would know how special you are to me," said Mr. Salam, sipping his glass of iced tea and lemonade.

"Thank you, Jady. Jenks said his father really likes Mickey Mantle," Ali said.

"Ah yes, the angry man in the wheelchair. I have not spoken to him. I usually see him when I watch baseball with my American friends at the Cozy Inn," said Mr. Salam, smiling. "They forgive me, even though I am a Yankees fan instead of Dodgers or Angels."

Ali sat down next to his grandfather as the sunset gave way to evening. "The other men from the mosque…" he said, thinking out loud.

"Yes?" Mr. Salam took another sip of his cool drink.

"They do not watch baseball with you?" asked Ali.

Mr. Salam cleaned his spectacles, and a neighbor dog howled at a distant siren. "Oh, they think I should not go there. But we live in America now, the land of the free. I see no harm in it. I do not drink alcohol, and I sit in the restaurant, separated from the bar, but I can still see the big screens," he explained.

"Yes, Grandfather," said Ali.

"They need to learn that there is a time for spiritual reflection and enlightenment, and then there is a time for baseball." Mr. Salam smiled and wiped his spectacles before putting them back in his pocket. Ali smiled back.

"You must have had a good reason to give away that card," said Mr. Salam.

"I think so, Jady," Ali said.

Mr. Salam stood up and checked on his hives one last time before darkness descended upon his city garden.

Ali jumped up from his chair, having remembered a new bee fact. "I learned that the honeybee protects the hive and especially the queen. But the worker bees can sting only once," he said with pride.

"Yes, she dies when she uses her stinger," said Mr. Salam.

"That is sad," Ali said, thinking about death.

"Sacrifice," said Ali's grandfather. He emphasized the word with his index finger pointed up in the air. He gave Ali a pat on the shoulder, which Ali always found comforting.

"Honeycomb made by honeybees is made of perfectly constructed hexagons that waste no space," Mr. Salam said.

"I read that honeycomb structures are used in the aerospace industry to maximize strength and minimize weight," said Ali with exuberance.

"You are learning, Ali," said Mr. Salam proudly.

The old man bent over in pain, causing Ali to worry.

"Jady?" asked a nervous Ali.

The old man patted Ali on the shoulder to reassure him that he was all right. He straightened up again and continued. "They are brilliant builders. Honeybees also have great memories. They memorize locations of flowers and where to get the most nectar and pollen," said Mr. Salam.

"Very smart," said Ali.

"Amazing creatures," said Mr. Salam.

Ali had still more bee facts he needed to share. "And the queen—she lays thousands of eggs a day to make more workers," he said as he helped his grandfather put away the tools amid the increased traffic noise.

"Ah, the queen, yes. She can live up to five years before she is replaced. The workers decide when to replace her. The queen also decides how aggressive the hive will be," explained Mr. Salam.

"How do they decide?" asked Ali.

"When the queen is old and tired." Mr. Salam felt a twinge in his back and smiled at Ali.

"So the workers are in charge, even though the queen is the queen?" the boy asked.

"Yes, Ali," answered Mr. Salam in the twilight of the day. He and Ali prepared to go inside.

"I know a queen bee," said Ali.

"What?" asked Mr. Salam.

"A friend. A girl."

"Girlfriend?" asked the old man with a twinkle in his eye.

"No, just a friend," Ali said as his grandfather smiled some more.

"Good to know," said Mr. Salam. The bees were asleep in their hives, and Ali and his grandfather took one last look at their garden before they stepped inside their modest home.

"I am so lucky to have you, Jady. You teach me so much," said Ali. He hugged his grandfather.

Surprised, the old man let out a gentle laugh. "We are both lucky. Knowledge is free for those who listen and learn," he said. The screen door to their house closed with a snap behind them, and a few dogs in the distance howled at unfamiliar shadows in the night.

ALL TOGETHER NOW

CHEWING ON his pencil in deep thought the next day, Ali carefully considered the best way to present his bee facts. Lupe looked around their shabby public school classroom and sighed. Ali and Lupe had asked Ms. Waters for permission to use her classroom to work on their project for a while.

"Jenks tried to switch earlier, but Ms. Waters forced him to be in our group," said Lupe. Jenks had not been at school that day.

"Why?" asked Ali.

"He's sad. Nobody else really likes him. He doesn't have any real friends," Lupe said with a frown.

"I did not know that," Ali said.

"He's angry too," Lupe said.

Ms. Waters came in to check on them, smiled, and, with reluctance, returned to her meeting.

"Is it because you did not want to be his girl-friend?" asked Ali.

"No...well, maybe. No, that's not it," Lupe said.

"I did not really want you to be my girlfriend—" said Ali.

Lupe interrupted him. "What? Why not?"

"I just wanted to be your friend."

"Really?"

Ali nodded. "I think you are wonderful," he said.

Lupe hugged him. "Ah, *gracias*. I think you're wonderful too," she said. She looked at Ali seriously. "His dad's heart is sick from what he saw."

"Jenks's father?"

"*Sí*." Lupe continued to work on her lettering for the project.

"The war?" asked Ali.

"Yeah." Lupe sprang to her feet. "Hey, I just thought of something! Maybe you should ask your grandfather to talk to Jenks's dad. What do you think?"

Ali thought for a few moments and a few moments more, which prompted Lupe to snap her fingers in front of him.

"Where do you go?" asked Lupe.

"What?"

"You zone out," she said.

"I remember things," Ali said as Lupe sat back down again.

"Like what?" she asked.

"I think about before I came here, to America." Ali grew slightly uncomfortable and stopped writing in his notebook.

"Oh," said Lupe.

"Sometimes I have bad dreams," he said.

A few students ran by the door, chasing one another and screaming. Ms. Waters, who had come back to her classroom to get something, yelled at the other students to settle down and stop running.

"I understand," said Lupe sympathetically.

Ms. Waters got some papers from her desk and smiled. "Everything all right?" she asked.

"Yeah, we're making progress," Lupe said.

"OK, you two can stay for another fifteen minutes. I have to go home eventually," said Ms.

Waters, smiling.

"Thanks," said Lupe.

"Thank you," Ali said.

As Ms. Waters left the classroom, another student on a skateboard zoomed by and almost hit her.

"Are you kidding me? Riding a skateboard on school property? I don't think so!" yelled Ms. Waters.

Lupe giggled and looked at a serious-faced Ali. Lupe sensed that something was making him sad.

"When I was driving downtown with my grandfather, we saw some homeless people, and…" Ali began to choke up.

"What is it?" asked Lupe.

"A lot of kids in Iraq were homeless because their parents died in the war." Ali fought his tears.

"That's terrible," said Lupe sympathetically.

"They had to beg, and the girls were taken as slaves," he said.

Lupe touched Ali's hand as he spoke.

"The insurgents came and tried to recruit the children," he said.

"To fight?"

"Yes, against the crusaders…the Americans," Ali said.

Lupe looked upset. "But they're just kids," she said.

"I know," said Ali with deep sadness.

Lupe touched Ali's hand again. "Is that what happened to you?" she asked tenderly.

Ali paused and thought deeply. "Yes, all because of the insurgents. Some people call them terrorists," he said.

"That's who we're fighting, right?" asked Lupe.

"Yes," he said.

"Are we winning?"

"I do not know," Ali said in despair.

"I'm sorry your parents are gone," said Lupe softly.

Ali tried to fight back his emotions. "I was an orphan. I had nothing, just bad dreams. I went to live with my grandfather. Last year we came to America."

"I'm glad you're safe now," Lupe said, smiling.

"Me too. My grandfather is the best. I just wish I could forget what happened, but I need to..." Ali choked up again.

Lupe put her hand gently on his shoulder. "You don't have to," she said.

"No, I want to tell you," said Ali.

"OK."

He took out the photo of his parents and showed it to Lupe. She looked at it with teary eyes, and then handed it back to him.

Ali mustered all his strength to try not to break down completely. "My parents—they were blown up. We were just shopping in the market, and the whole place blew up. Nothing left. But I survived." He paused to catch his breath. "Not sure why. Why me?"

Lupe gave Ali a bear hug as Ali tried hard to suppress his emotions. "You're not alone," said Lupe.

"I know. You are right," said Ali. He wiped his tears and put the photo back in his pocket.

"I sometimes have nightmares too," Lupe said.

"You do?" Ali welcomed a shift in the conversation.

"Yeah. Actually two nightmares that I have over and over."

"What are they?" asked Ali.

Lupe became sad as she thought of her nightmares, so Ali put his hand on hers.

"One is about my mama," she said. She tried hard

not to choke up. "ICE officers come to our house—"

"ICE?" asked Ali.

"Immigration and Customs Enforcement. Yeah, they come to our house and take Mama away in the middle of the night, and there's nothing I can do. I'm, like, paralyzed and can't move, and my little brother and sister are crying," she said as tears rolled down her cheeks.

"Can they do that?" asked Ali.

"Maybe. She's not documented."

"Oh, but she is your mom," said Ali.

Lupe shrugged her shoulders. "But I was born here, and my brother and sister too," she said, wiping away her tears.

"I will help you," said Ali.

Lupe grinned, and they both sat in silence for a moment.

"What is the other nightmare?" he asked.

"The other nightmare is where I can't breathe," she said as the school janitor walked by slowly with his mop and bucket, humming some forgotten song.

"Why?" asked Ali.

"I have stupid asthma. I'm allergic to lots of things: cats, dogs, horses, insect bites, *ai, ai, ai*," Lupe said.

"I did not know," said Ali with surprise.

"I don't tell people. I don't want them to feel sorry for me, stop me from doing things I want to do, or treat me differently," she said defiantly.

"I never noticed it," said Ali.

"I'm strong. I don't let my asthma stop me. Never, ever." Lupe was even more defiant.

"We have to keep going, day by day, no matter what," Ali said.

Lupe paused. Then she said, "You're right. By the way, did you like my idea?"

"What idea?"

Lupe slapped his arm playfully. "¡*Ai!* To have your grandfather speak to Mr. Hooper, Jenks's dad," she reminded him.

"I will ask him," said Ali, rubbing his arm. A few minutes later, both Ali and Lupe packed up their project materials and headed home. It had been an emotional day—a successful day.

9

JIHAD

ALI WALKED home from school, noticing all the cracks in the sidewalk, skipping over them, and whistling a tuneless song. The same dog that barked at him in the morning barked at him as he returned home in the afternoon.

Ali thought about his friendship with Lupe, which made him smile, and about his troubled past in Iraq, which took his smile away. He walked past Mr. Mood's store and waved at Mr. Mood, who waved back as he swept his storefront.

"Hello, Ali," said Mr. Mood cheerfully as he leaned on his push broom.

A little bit farther, he strode past the Madrigal children, who were spilling out into their yard, as noisy as ever.

Ali enjoyed the sound of families. He stopped for

a moment in front of the Turners' dark and closed-up home to see whether he could see a sign of life. Did the curtain move? No, just his imagination.

Ali neared his home. Señor, the fat, lazy gray tabby cat, greeted Ali with a loud meow and plopped down on the sidewalk to be petted—his usual custom. Ali loved Señor and considered him a friend. He also loved his after-school routine. It made him feel comfortable and safe. Finally, Ali arrived home, and, naturally, his grandfather could be found in the garden.

Later, Ali helped by weeding the vegetable garden while his grandfather worked with his bees, checking the hives and using his smoker to calm the hardworking insects.

The neighbors were playing mariachi music on their old hi-fi stereo with speakers that crackled and hummed. The bees buzzed all around them. Ali had been rather quiet since he came home from school, and his grandfather had noticed.

"What are you thinking about, Ali?" asked Mr. Salam.

"The war," said Ali as he continued to hoe the vegetable garden.

"Ah yes," said Mr. Salam as he peered over his spectacles.

Ali felt a swell of emotion as he thought about what had happened.

"I know you saw this terrible thing, your mother and father…" said the old man tenderly.

Ali stopped working. "I cannot get it out of my thoughts," he said.

"That is normal. It has only been a few years," said Mr. Salam. Using his cane to steady himself, he walked over to Ali.

"And Grandmother too. Disappeared," Ali said.

Mr. Salam put his weathered hand on Ali's shoulder. "Their spirits are whole; they were innocents.

The prophet Muhammad taught us that three things continue to benefit a believer even after death: their charity, which they have given and which continues to benefit others; their knowledge, which they have left behind; and supplication on their behalf by a righteous child."

Ali gave him a hug. "I miss them all so much," he said mournfully.

"Always remember. Remember your mother and father's sacrifice. Just like the sacrifice of the bees for the colony. Always remember," said Mr. Salam.

Ali and his grandfather stood side by side for a few minutes in silence, looking at the garden and beehives as the sun sank low on the horizon.

"Why is there war? Why do these people kill each other?" asked Ali plaintively.

"They have run out of ideas. War is a bankruptcy of ideas." Ali's grandfather tapped his cane on the ground for emphasis.

"Why did they kill Mother and Father?" asked Ali.

Mr. Salam once again put his hand on Ali's shoulder. "Your father was a soldier," he explained.

"A policeman," Ali said, correcting his grandfather and shaking his head.

"A military policeman," Mr. Salam said. "The insurgents want to create chaos, anger, and fear." There was a hint of righteous anger in his voice.

"I do not understand," said Ali.

Mr. Salam moved over to one of the two rusty garden chairs and sat down slowly. A distant siren wailed, and a few neighborhood dogs joined in the howling chorus.

"When people are confused, angry, and afraid, they can be more easily controlled," Ali's grandfather said.

"The insurgents tried to recruit us," said Ali.

"They prey on the young and those who are suffering," Mr. Salam said.

"They told me the crusaders killed my parents," said Ali. His memories flooded back into his mind and stirred his emotions.

"That is not true. The insurgents say they speak for Allah and that they are following the Koran. They do neither. They are zealots following themselves and their own selfish interests." Again the old man tapped his cane on the ground for emphasis.

Ali felt anger when he thought about people using religion that way. He went to sit next to his grandfather. Mr. Salam grabbed a glass of iced tea and lemonade from the rusted, round wire table placed between the garden chairs and drank.

"Ah," said Mr. Salam. "Delicious. Arnold Palmer knew his refreshments. A brilliant combination, iced tea and lemonade." He smiled.

"What about jihad?" asked Ali as his grandfather placed his glass back on the rickety table.

"Like Christianity, Islam permits fighting in self-defense. But there are strict rules: do not harm innocents, and do not destroy crops, trees, or livestock. Good people must be prepared to risk their lives in a righteous cause," explained Mr. Salam.

"Does that mean we have to kill?" asked Ali.

"Self-defense is not killing, Ali. It is said, 'Fight in the cause of God against those who fight you, but do not transgress limits. God does not love transgressors. If they seek peace, you seek peace. And trust in God, for he is the one that hears and knows all things.'" Mr. Salam looked up into the darkening sky.

"So we only fight when we have to? No other choice?" asked Ali.

"Jihad is both an internal and external struggle. Internally we fight against selfish desires, to find inner peace. Externally we may fight against enemies who threaten the innocent and destroy life and livelihoods, so that we can all live in peace," Mr. Salam said.

"I think I understand, Jady. But what do I do with this anger?" asked Ali.

Mr. Salam patted Ali on the shoulder. "It is normal to be angry when you have had loved ones stolen from you. The time will come when you can do something, but not now."

Ali brought out the photograph of his parents and looked at it as his grandfather spoke. "I want to do something," Ali said.

"It is said, 'He is not strong and powerful who throws people down, but he is strong who withholds himself from anger,'" the old man said.

Ali thought for a few moments. "It is so hard."

"The best jihad is self-control. We must all choose our own paths," advised Mr. Salam.

Ali stood up and paced a bit before he spoke. "Are we winning?"

"What? Winning?" asked Mr. Salam.

"The war," Ali clarified.

"Oh."

"Against the insurgents," Ali said.

Mr. Salam stood up with some difficulty, due to his arthritic knees. "There is no winning."

"But you said sometimes we have to fight against our enemies."

"Yes," said Mr. Salam.

This answer confused Ali. He put away his photograph and grabbed the hoe and began to weed the garden.

"If one wins, another loses, yes?" asked Mr. Salam. He retrieved his smoker and began inspecting his hives.

"I guess so," said Ali.

"If both win, no one loses," Mr. Salam said.

"OK."

"We must help our enemies see the truth. The weapons we can use are logic, compassion, common goals, shared suffering, and love," said Ali's grandfather.

This caused Ali to think deeply as he leaned on his hoe.

"One war leads to another as people seek revenge against their enemies. War hardens the heart and takes part of a person's soul in the process. The warrior returns home transformed. Some have called this 'soldier's heart.' Warriors need healing, but the healing never comes, only more war," said Mr. Salam.

The bees buzzed around his head, and twilight descended on their city garden. Ali finished his weeding, put the hoe away, and returned to help his grandfather before it became too dark to work. The neighbors' hi-fi stereo now gave way to loud canned laughter from a TV comedy show they were watching.

"Grandfather, Lupe had an idea," said Ali.

"Lupe?" asked Mr. Salam.

"Lupe, my friend."

"Ah, the girl who is a friend, not a girlfriend." Mr. Salam grinned. There was a twinkle in his eye.

"She said maybe it was a good idea if you talked to Mr. Hooper, Jenks's father," Ali said.

Ali's grandfather thought for a moment as the sound of a distant siren came closer. "That *is* a good idea," he said enthusiastically.

"I want to help."

"I know you do, Ali. We can all learn from the

honeybees and how they work together in harmony toward a common goal of survival for the community. We need such unity in Iraq and everywhere, all of us working together in peace. *Inshallah*," said Mr. Salam as he gazed at the multicolored sunset and wrapped his arm gently around Ali.

Ali rested his head against his beloved grandfather—safe at home.

ORPHANS

JENKS SWUNG his bat at the community baseball field a few days later.

"And Jenks Hooper hits the game-winning home run in game seven of the World Series. The crowd goes wild," he said as he smiled. It was a warm, sunny afternoon. Someone had worked on the field, so the smell of newly mown grass filled the air.

Mr. Hooper slowly rolled up to his son as a road worker began jackhammering a few blocks away. This noise startled Mr. Hooper, angering him.

"Watch the curveball today. Don't strike out like you did last time," warned Mr. Hooper.

"Dad, it was hard to—"

Jenks's father interrupted him. "Excuses, right? Are you gonna give me excuses?" His voice was angry.

"No, Dad, but—"

His father cut him off again. "Be smarter up there at the plate. You own it. Don't back down."

"I didn't," said Jenks sheepishly as his dad rolled around him.

"Ah, don't embarrass yourself. I hardly ever struck out. I got on base, stole a base, everything. It's easy. Just have to be more aggressive." Mr. Hooper stopped circling his son and calmed down. He looked at the ground, feeling sadness replace his burning anger. He could not control his anger, especially with his son.

Some other kids had arrived and were laughing and playing catch. Mr. Hooper wished that Jenks could be so carefree and happy. In the back of his mind, he knew why Jenks could not be like the other kids.

"Dad, I have something for you," said Jenks with a careful smile.

"What?"

Jenks reached into his baseball bag and handed his father the Mickey Mantle baseball card.

Mr. Hooper examined the card for a few moments and appeared to be carried away to another place and another time. He even smiled momentarily, but anger pushed away his joy. "You stole it!" he yelled.

"No," Jenks said, trying to stand up to his father.

"What did I tell you about stealing?" Mr. Hooper's face grew flushed with anger.

"I swear I didn't," pleaded Jenks.

"Likely story," said Mr. Hooper.

Jenks thought for a moment or two. "Ali gave it to me," he said, to his father's surprise.

"The Taliban boy?"

"No, he's from Iraq," Jenks said.

"Who would give away a Mickey Mantle card?"

asked Mr. Hooper as more kids arrived and began warming up.

"He did. He gave it to me," Jenks said.

"Why?" Mr. Hooper was growing frustrated.

"I don't know."

"I don't believe it," Mr. Hooper said.

Jenks was trying hard to stand up for himself, but sadness overtook him, and he began to tear up.

His son's tears both angered and embarrassed Mr. Hooper. He rolled farther away from the others on the field and dragged Jenks with him.

"Why don't you ever believe me?" the boy asked.

"Because you lie."

"Only a few times, but I promised you—"

His father cut him off. "Why would someone give you anything?" Mr. Hooper tried to keep his voice down and not bring attention to him and his son.

"Please believe me," Jenks pleaded. He began to cry harder.

Mr. Hooper looked all around before he spoke. "Knock it off," he said.

"I'm sorry, Dad," said Jenks. He tried to stop crying.

"Man up! This is nothing; the world will eat you up if you act like that. I was only nineteen when I lost my first soldier. Too busy crying and not doing my job cost him his life," said Mr. Hooper with restrained anger.

"Dad, I try," said Jenks.

"Don't try. Just do it. What have I taught you?"

"A man fights—"

His father interrupted him. "Louder!" he demanded.

"A man fights for what he—"

"Louder!" insisted Mr. Hooper.

"A man fights for what he believes in, no matter what!" yelled Jenks. The shouting drew the attention of some of the other boys practicing on the field.

"OK," said Mr. Hooper calmly.

For a few moments, Jenks and his dad remained silent. A loud jet flew overhead, and the voices of the other players carried across the field. Jenks struggled with rising and uncomfortable emotions.

"I want you to believe…in me, Dad," said Jenks.

Mr. Hooper withdrew in silence, turning his wheelchair away from his son. Jenks wiped away his tears when Ali arrived.

"Maybe someday you'll get to play, but not today," snapped Jenks. Ali sat on the bench, and Jenks ran out to the field.

After a few moments, Mr. Hooper returned and rolled next to Ali by the rusty chain-link fence near the dugout.

A stray dog barked as a few of the boys chased him. The dog had grabbed a glove in a game of keep-away and saw no reason to give up easily. The sun was baking the baseball field, but the dugout provided some shady relief.

"You Ali?" asked Mr. Hooper.

"Yes," answered Ali. "Mr. Hooper?"

"Yeah." Mr. Hooper acted calm but felt guilty about what he had said to his son.

"I think we will win today," said Ali.

"He's really a little jerk sometimes," said Mr. Hooper.

The cross talk confused Ali. "Excuse me?" he asked.

"My son, Jenks," clarified Mr. Hooper.

"I am trying to make friends with him." Ali

smiled.

"It's my fault, I suppose," Mr. Hooper said.

Ali thought and then smiled. "We all choose our own path," he said.

The two sat in silence for a few moments before Mr. Hooper retrieved a baseball card from the army medical bag he always wore around his shoulder. He held it carefully and with reverence.

"Jenks said you gave him this card," he said.

"Yes, I wanted him to have it," said Ali.

Mr. Hooper felt conflicted. He wanted not to like Ali, but Ali could not be kinder or friendlier. "Well…we can't accept it," he said.

"Why?" asked Ali.

Mr. Hooper's hands were shaking as he tried hard to contain his conflicting emotions. The ice-cream man strolled by with his cart and jingling bell. "Where'd you get it?" he asked.

"My grandfather gave it to me. He loves baseball," answered Ali enthusiastically.

"He's a Yankees fan?" asked Mr. Hooper.

"Yes," said Ali proudly.

Mr. Hooper thought for a moment. "I think I've

seen him at the Cozy Inn. Haven't talked to him. Usually I keep to myself."

"Baseball is what he loves most about America," explained Ali.

Mr. Hooper came close to smiling. "Me too. I used to play. I played in high school. Quite a hitter, good pitcher too, and I could run like..." Mr. Hooper's smile faded as he looked down at his paralyzed legs.

"Grandfather would like it if I loved baseball too," said Ali.

"Does he know you gave the card away?" asked

Mr. Hooper.

"Yes."

"He's not mad at you?"

"I do not think so," said Ali.

Mr. Hooper gazed at the card with admiration and a moment of joy. "Mickey Mantle's an American icon, a hero. My favorite baseball player," he said.

Unbeknownst to Mr. Hooper and Ali, Jenks had approached and was listening.

Mr. Hooper thought some more and tried to hand the card to Ali. "You should give it back to him."

Ali would not take it back. He shook his head. "I do not want it back."

Mr. Hooper put his hand back down on his lap. Deep in thought, he looked at the card. "Jenks told me you're from Iraq," he said.

"Yes," said Ali.

"I was in Iraq." There was great pain in his voice.

Ali felt he could tell Mr. Hooper what had happened. "My parents were murdered. My grandmother disappeared," he said solemnly.

"You lost your whole family?" asked Mr. Hooper.

"Yes, except for my grandfather," said Ali.

Mr. Hooper looked up and down. With great difficulty, he suppressed his emotions. "I lost guys in my unit, most of them. Some over there, some here…suicide…they're my family."

"I understand."

"I think you do," Mr. Hooper said.

They both sat in silence for a few moments. An approaching siren screamed in the distance, and a stray dog barked.

Mr. Hooper slapped his legs. "Came back like this. Not sure why I got to live."

"We are here for a reason, I think," suggested Ali.

"Yeah, I suppose," Mr. Hooper said.

They both thought back to their experiences in Iraq—that place where they shared so much pain.

"We left everything behind there," said Mr. Hooper wistfully.

"Yes," Ali said.

"We're both orphans of that war," said Mr. Hooper. Ali smiled at him.

The reflective moment was broken as Jenks announced his presence by accidentally dropping his bat on the sidewalk behind the backstop. "You tried to give the card back?" he yelled.

"He did not—" Ali said.

Jenks cut him off. "Why can't you talk to me like that, Dad? Like you talk to him!" He shouted loudly enough that the other boys took notice.

"Son, I—" Mr. Hooper tried to explain, but Jenks persisted.

"Don't you love me?" Jenks was yelling, but his voice quavered.

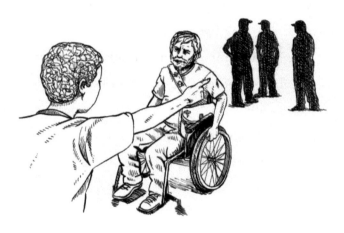

Mr. Hooper stared sympathetically at his son, whose heart was overflowing with anger and sorrow. Mr. Hooper tried to reach out to him, but Jenks ran off. He began to shake uncontrollably in his wheel-chair. His tears flowed for the first time in many years as his clenched fists began to loosen. Mr. Hooper was finally releasing some of his anger and frustration that he had kept bottled up since the war. Ali sat quietly.

A stray dog howled mournfully in the distance, and some crows quarreled over a candy wrapper as Mr. Hooper, weeping, with his head hung low, wheeled off the field to see whether he could find his son and possibly repair their relationship.

11

THE COZY INN

LATER IN THE evening, at a well-worn table at the Cozy Inn Sports Bar and Grill, Mr. Hooper sat alone, drinking a beer in a dark corner. An eclectic mix of people watched games on several smaller-screen TVs and regaled one another with tales of work and life that day. One large-screen TV, strategically placed, could be seen from both the bar and restaurant sides.

The bar music made conversation difficult, but Mr. Hooper didn't notice, since he sat alone in silent thought. He flipped his 82nd Airborne Division challenge coin, a cherished gift he had received from his unit when he was injured in the war, over and over in his hand.

Mr. Hooper heard a distinctive laugh that broke his concentration. He looked up and saw Ali's grandfather, using a cane for support, slowly making his way into the restaurant. The old man laughed again and waved to a few folks who recognized him. He had a broad, infectious smile and good nature that the bar patrons seemed to enjoy. The old man headed to Mr. Hooper's table. The music faded as the big-screen TV came to life.

"Are the Yankees playing?" asked Ali's grandfather, already knowing the answer.

"Yeah, about to start," replied Mr. Hooper. He looked at the old man, who sat down across from him at the table. Mr. Hooper was uncomfortable seeing someone in traditional Arab clothing, because it brought back terrible images of war that he had tried hard to suppress.

However, the old man was disarming and friendly, which countered those traumatic images and brought back some good memories of Iraqis he had worked with in Fallujah.

They both had a good view of the big screen.

"What an excellent day. What do they say? Baseball, hot dogs, and..." He paused to remember and placed his cane over the back of an extra chair.

"Chevrolet," Mr. Hooper said.

"Ah yes," said Ali's grandfather. "Chevrolet."

"I'm more of a Ford man," said Mr. Hooper, looking up from his beer.

"As am I. Family company, you know."

Mr. Hooper nodded in agreement. "You're Ali's grandfather, right?" he asked.

"Yes, Mohammad Salam." Mr. Salam extended his hand, and Mr. Hooper, taken by surprise, shook it a bit awkwardly. Mr. Salam found it odd but true that most people were amazed by his graciousness and kindness.

"Morgan Hooper," said Mr. Hooper.

"I am very pleased to meet you, Mr. Hooper, officially," said Ali's grandfather, flashing his radiant smile.

"Likewise, officially," said Mr. Hooper politely. He searched for something to say, since people did not usually sit next to him at the Cozy Inn. Unfortunately, angry people often inadvertently pushed away those who could help them once again find joy in their lives. Mr. Salam, luckily for Mr. Hooper, could help him.

"'Salam'—that means peace, right?" asked Mr.

Hooper.

"That is correct," answered Mr. Salam. Mr. Hooper smiled.

"Your grandson tries hard. To play, that is. He's a good boy," said Mr. Hooper.

"Thank you. Yes, he is learning, but it is a difficult game. A great American game," responded Mr. Salam.

"Yeah, true," said Mr. Hooper.

They both paused to watch the big screen.

"So you're a Yankees fan?" asked Mr. Hooper.

"Most certainly. I became a Yankees fan in Iraq," replied Mr. Salam.

"Ali told me you're from Iraq," Mr. Hooper said.

"Baquba. But now this is our home, Los Angeles," said the old man, smiling.

They both watched the screen a bit more.

"You served in the war?" asked Mr. Salam as the server brought an Arnold Palmer for him and a bowl of pretzels for both of them.

"Yeah, that's why I'm like this. Caught a piece of shrapnel in Fallujah," said Mr. Hooper.

"I was proud to work with the US Army," said

Mr. Salam.

"I was in the army. Eighty-Second Airborne. I was a medic." Mr. Hooper showed his challenge coin to Mr. Salam, who held it briefly, smiled, and gave it back.

"You are a brave man," said Mr. Salam earnestly as Mr. Hooper put the challenge coin in his medical bag.

"I don't know about that," said Mr. Hooper. They both took sips from their drinks, ate pretzels, and watched the game silently until Mr. Hooper pointed to the screen.

"Ah, that was a strike. C'mon, man!" he yelled.

"That umpire is in need of vision correction," the old man said. They both smiled, and Mr. Hooper came close to laughing.

"What did you do with the army?" asked Mr. Hooper.

"Interpreter, working with Colonel Bill for the Ministry of the Interior," answered Mr. Salam as he grabbed a few more pretzels.

"Wow, the police. That's dangerous work," said Mr. Hooper, impressed.

"Yes, it could be, but everywhere in Iraq is dangerous," replied the old man. They watched the screen again, and Mr. Salam shook his head. "The Yankees will have to hit today because their defense is certainly most pitiful," he commented. They both smiled.

Mr. Hooper finished his beer and motioned to the server.

"Get you a beer?" he asked the old man.

Mr. Salam looked at Mr. Hooper and smiled.

"Oh, sorry, you don't drink. Forbidden in Islam, right?" Mr. Hooper ordered just one beer. The server pointed to the old man's glass.

"Refill?" asked the server.

"No thank you," said Mr. Salam, who then turned back to Mr. Hooper.

"Not expressly forbidden, but the Koran does advise against alcohol and games of chance," answered Mr. Salam.

"I bet," said Mr. Hooper. After he realized what he had said, both he and Mr. Salam laughed.

"Arnold Palmer," said Mr. Salam.

"Huh?" said Mr. Hooper.

"My drink," said the old man as Mr. Hooper smiled.

"Oh yeah, they're good," said Mr. Hooper who began to fidget in his wheelchair. Soon, they were watching the game again, but Mr. Hooper could not stop his intrusive thoughts of war.

"I lost some guys over there, friends and some soldiers I could've saved," Mr. Hooper confided.

"I am sorry for those losses. War always takes, never gives," said Mr. Salam solemnly.

"I know you lost family."

"Yes, it is most sad. But Ali and I have each other. *Alhamdulillah*," Mr. Salam said as he looked up.

Mr. Hooper thought about this and felt guilty again about how he had treated his son earlier. The old man noticed.

"Yeah," said Mr. Hooper, with a tinge of sadness.

"Your son, Jenks—he is a fine ballplayer," said Mr. Salam.

"Yes, he is. I…" Mr. Hooper choked up a bit.

"We have good boys. It is not easy to raise children alone," Mr. Salam continued.

"His mother tries when he visits her, but she's

kind of a mess," explained Mr. Hooper.

"I see." The old man was sympathetic.

"And so am I," said Mr. Hooper, attempting to hide his emotions. Mr. Salam glanced at the game action on the big screen at that moment and responded vociferously.

"Yes!" yelled Mr. Salam. Confused, Mr. Hooper thought the old man was agreeing with him.

"Huh?" he said. He looked at the screen, and Mr. Salam pointed to the game action.

"Oh," said Mr. Hooper. They both laughed at the momentary misunderstanding.

"Home run!" yelled Mr. Salam.

"I guess that makes up for those base-running mistakes," said Mr. Hooper.

"The problem with the Yankees today is that they make too many wrong mistakes," said Mr. Salam with a playful grin.

Mr. Hooper understood the reference immediately. "Yogi Berra."

Mr. Hooper and the old man said simultaneously, laughing. After a few moments and more sips of their drinks, Mr. Salam turned to Mr. Hooper with an earnest look.

"You are not a mess. I see you as a very brave man who has paid a high price in war as part of a noble effort," he said.

Mr. Hooper began to choke up.

"Your son sees that too. Believe me."

"You really think so?"

"Yes. We bring the war home with us—not on purpose, of course, but we do—so our children must also face the consequences of war. We want to protect them from the war, but, in so doing, we close ourselves off from them," continued Mr. Salam.

Mr. Hooper reflected deeply on this wisdom. "Yeah." Tears began to run down his face.

The old man noticed and put his weathered hand on top of Mr. Hooper's hand. "From shared suffering comes understanding, and from understanding comes peace," he said.

"Yeah." Mr. Hooper struggled to maintain his well-practiced stoicism. After a few moments, they both turned their attention once again to the TV screen.

"Double play. A pitcher's best friend, as Colonel

Bill used to say," Mr. Salam said.

"It sure is," agreed Mr. Hooper. After another moment or two, he took the Mickey Mantle card out of his well-worn medical bag. "I can't keep this," he said respectfully as Mr. Salam admired the old card.

"Ali gave the Mickey Mantle card to your boy," the old man said.

"And Jenks gave it to me, hoping that I would..." Mr. Hooper began to break down.

"I understand. This card means something special to all of us," Mr. Salam said.

"You should have it back," insisted Mr. Hooper.

The old man thought for a moment. "I believe the card should be shared by all of us," he suggested.

"What?"

The old man took another sip of his Arnold Palmer before proceeding. "Since Colonel Bill gave me his Mickey Mantle card, each owner has realized that the true joy and value of the card is as a symbol of kindness and friendship. I am certain the Mickey Mantle card will have a place of honor at your home and will represent our friendship. When Ali and I come to visit you and your boy, we can see and share in your joy," said Mr. Salam.

Surprised and grateful, Mr. Hooper remained silent for a moment as he dried his eyes with his shirt sleeve. "I don't know what to say, but thank you." He continued to fight his deep emotions, watching the game wistfully as he searched for something more to say.

"The Yankees sure could use him now," said Mr. Hooper.

"Yes," agreed Mr. Salam.

"We could all use a hero like Mickey these days."

"Yes, he was a fearless and talented player, but the most interesting thing about Mickey Mantle is the heroism he showed at the end of his life. That is when he realized what alcohol had done to his career, to his image with his fans, and to his family. In his final years, he could face that honestly and with remorse and true courage," said the old man.

Mr. Hooper thought intensely for a few moments and watched the game. During a commercial break, he slid his beer away and prepared to go by turning away from the table. "I'm sorry. Please excuse me, Mr. Salam," he said respectfully.

"Will you not stay for the game?" asked Mr. Salam.

"I better get home. Thank you," said Mr. Hooper. He thought about Jenks sitting alone at home.

The old man put his hand on Mr. Hooper's shoulder as a sign of friendship and respect. "*As-salamu alaikum*, my warrior friend. It was an honor to meet you, officially," said Mr. Salam proudly.

"Thank you. I'm glad I've finally met you," said Mr. Hooper. Emotion strained his vocal chords.

The old man shook Mr. Hooper's hand and watched him roll away. As Mr. Salam reached for the pretzels, he felt a sharp pain in his chest. The old man winced and held his chest for a moment, but then the pain passed. He wiped the sweat from his brow with his napkin, took a deep breath as he looked up, and then smiled. He took another big sip of his cool drink, grabbed a handful of pretzels, and continued to watch the Yankees on the big screen.

REDEMPTION

HAZY AND warm weather greeted the ballplayers at the baseball field the next day. The marine layer had descended on Southern California in what locals called the June gloom. By afternoon, the cloud layer would lift, and a bright, sunny day would magically appear. It was typical weather for Los Angeles in early summer.

At a house bordering the ball field, kids were screaming and laughing at a birthday party, complete with an inflatable bounce house and blaring mariachi music. Celebrations of life were important for old and young and for rich and poor.

Ali, Mr. Salam, and Lupe were all standing together, ready for the game to begin.

"The coach says I get to play right field today, batting ninth," Ali said with great pride.

"*Ai*, that's great," said Lupe enthusiastically.

"Remember what I told you, Ali. Slow the ball down. Use your bee vision," Mr. Salam said.

"Yes, Grandfather," said Ali.

Lupe thought for a moment. "*¿Que?* Bee vision?"

"Honeybees have five eyes, three small ones on top of the head and two big compound eyes in front, each with six thousand nine hundred lenses," explained Ali. He pounded his fist into his glove.

"*Ai, ai, ai,*" said Lupe in amazement.

"They can see things we cannot. Bees can see ultraviolet light that helps them find nectar in flowers. If a bee sat down and watched a movie with you, she would not see continuous motion; she would see each individual frame. Bees can detect motion six times faster than humans," said Mr. Salam.

"Wow, bee vision," said Lupe, nodding. Bee facts both impressed and overwhelmed her.

Ali grabbed a bat and took slow practice swings. "You cannot hit what you cannot see," he said.

"Walter Johnson, great Hall of Fame pitcher, not a Yankee," said Mr. Salam, smiling. He tilted his head and raised a finger in the air for added emphasis.

Jenks walked up to them, pushing his father in his wheelchair. Mr. Salam shook Mr. Hooper's hand as the boys prepared to take the field.

"Do you think you're ready?" asked Jenks.

"Ready for what?" asked Ali.

"To play right field."

"Yes, today I am ready."

"Good," said Jenks, cracking a hint of a smile.

Ali looked at Lupe and his grandfather, who smiled with encouragement.

Jenks pointed to right field, and Ali ran to take his position.

A few moments later, a loud buzzing sound came closer and closer. Everyone looked up and saw a massive swarm of bees approaching the ball field.

"What is that?" asked Lupe.

"It is a swarm of bees," answered Mr. Salam.

Lupe pointed at the sky. "Look, there they are," she said excitedly.

"Do not panic. They will leave you alone," advised Mr. Salam.

Jenks did not hear the advice and panicked. "Run!" he screamed.

Ali hurried back to them from right field, where the swarm had passed over his head.

"No! Stay still," Ali told Lupe and Jenks.

Lupe ran in fright. Jenks took after her and flailed away at the swarm of bees, which sensed his movements as a sign of aggression. Lupe and Jenks both ran in circles in full panic mode. Jenks swung his arms violently, trying to protect Lupe.

"Do not do that! It will make them aggressive!" yelled Mr. Salam.

"Lupe, Jenks, stop!" shouted Ali. He ran to his friends to get them to be still. It was too late. Lupe and Jenks had been stung multiple times. The swarm had moved on, and the fierce buzzing had stopped. They all stood in shock for a few moments before Lupe fell to the ground, gasping for breath.

Jenks freaked out. "Help her! She's dying!" he shouted.

Lupe continued to struggle to breathe, and she tried to stand up. Ali ran to her, followed by Mr. Salam and Mr. Hooper.

"Lupe needs help! She cannot breathe!" shouted Ali. Mr. Hooper wheeled up next to Lupe, whose lips had turned blue. Other kids and parents gathered around them.

"Back up and give her room!" yelled Mr. Hooper to the crowd. "Anaphylactic shock. She needs epinephrine," he said as he opened his medical bag.

"Mr. Hooper, you have to help her! Please!" pleaded Ali.

Mr. Hooper grabbed an EpiPen from his medical bag and struggled to reach Lupe on the ground. EpiPens containing epinephrine are used to treat severe, life-threatening allergic reactions.

He couldn't reach her from his wheelchair. Out of

desperation and frustrated by his paralysis, Mr. Hooper attempted to climb out of his wheelchair to reach Lupe, but Jenks gently touched his father's arm and looked at him. The next moment, Jenks grabbed the EpiPen and knelt next to Lupe.

"Son, you have to—"

Jenks interrupted him. "I know what to do, Dad. You taught me," he said confidently.

He removed the EpiPen from its tube container, pointed the orange tip downward, removed the blue cap, and swung and pushed the orange tip into her thigh. Everyone was silent and stared nervously at Lupe hoping for her swift recovery. She remained in a near fetal position for what seemed like an eternity as Ali and Jenks both blinked back tears. Finally, she began to move her arms and legs. Everyone heaved a sigh of relief as she began to feel better and sat up, breathing more normally.

A blaring siren approached. Jenks stood up, trembling and distraught. Ali hugged Lupe, who managed a little smile and coughed.

"The bees are not aggressive when they are swarming. They were looking for a new home," said

Ali with a break in his voice. His hands were shaking. Ali brought out the photograph of his parents as tears ran down his cheeks. The sirens reminded him of the aftermath of the explosion that killed his parents in Iraq.

"Sudden movement signaled aggression to them, so they attacked," Mr. Salam said.

"I didn't know. I'm sorry. I just wanted to help her," said a clearly upset Jenks. Everyone looked at him.

"Of course, you did not know. It is all right," said Mr. Salam warmly.

"Jenks...you did help me," said Lupe, recovering. They all stood in silence as the sirens grew closer and closer.

Mr. Hooper broke down and was racked with guilt. "It's my fault," he said through tears.

"No, Dad, no," said Jenks.

"I've been so mean," Mr. Hooper said.

Ali placed his hand on the man's shoulder.

"Jenks is a good boy," said Mr. Salam.

"I've been too angry, too afraid to care," continued Mr. Hooper.

"It's OK, Dad," said Jenks, who was also fighting tears.

"I haven't been much of a father for you, but I'll do better," said Mr. Hooper.

"Experience brings wisdom if love is the teacher," said Mr. Salam. He smiled and touched Mr. Hooper gently on the shoulder.

"Son, you have to let go of your anger. Don't be like me," said Mr. Hooper.

The emergency vehicles arrived, and the sirens stopped. All remained quiet for a moment.

"Dad, you don't get it. I want to be exactly like

you. You're my hero," said Jenks with great affection and pride.

"I love you, son," said Mr. Hooper affectionately as he hugged Jenks.

"I love you too, Dad," said Jenks with great emotion in his voice.

Lupe rose to her feet slowly with Ali's help. Ali and Lupe hugged Jenks and Mr. Hooper. Ali's grandfather smiled broadly.

Finally, the paramedics arrived, snapped open a gurney, and hurried to Lupe. As everyone was focusing on Lupe and the paramedics, Ali's grandfather, who looked a little pale, stumbled and held his chest. Mr. Hooper noticed.

"Are you OK, Mr. Salam?" asked Mr. Hooper.

Ali, who was still emotional from what had just happened, shifted his attention back to his grandfather and moved to his side. "Jady, are you sick?" he asked.

"I am fine," said Mr. Salam, smiling.

Mr. Hooper wasn't so sure. He motioned to one of the paramedics to check on the old man. Ali paced back and forth as Jenks stood nearby and looked on with great concern. Two of the paramedics placed Lupe on a gurney and moved her toward the ambulance. She looked at Mr. Salam and Ali, worried.

"We'll take him in and let the doc check him out," said one of the paramedics.

"Is that really necessary?" asked Mr. Salam.

"Just a precaution," said Mr. Hooper.

The old man smiled, and Ali, who was in tears, hugged him.

"I will be all right, Ali. Do not worry," said his grandfather. Mr. Hooper rolled over and patted Ali on the shoulder.

"He'll be fine," said Mr. Hooper. Ali was not convinced. He could not help but think of when he lost his parents. How would he make it without his grandfather?

The paramedics got another gurney for Ali's grandfather. At that moment, the sun finally broke through the late-morning haze, and the mariachi music played on.

Mr. Salam looked up at the sunny sky. "See, Ali, the sun is out, and all is well. *Inshallah*," he said.

Ali held his grandfather's hand and looked up,

closing his eyes. As he held on to the photograph of his parents in his other hand, Ali prayed silently, something he hadn't done in a long time.

13

ALL CREATURES GREAT AND SMALL

A FEW DAYS later, in a shabby public school classroom, the science fair had finally begun. Parents, teachers, siblings, and students all mingled and chatted until Ms. Waters eventually got everyone's attention.

"Welcome, everyone, to our class science fair. The students have worked incredibly hard in their groups to bring you their special projects," she said.

Everyone applauded politely.

"After the introductions, everyone is welcome to come and look at the displays up close and talk to our young scientists, who will explain their field studies and experiments in greater detail. We will start with a project presented by Ali, Lupe, and Jenks." Ms.

Waters beamed with pride as the three children nervously approached her. Ali was not his normal self. He was withdrawn and distant.

"What is it, Ali?" asked Ms. Waters.

Ali couldn't answer.

"His grandfather is in the hospital," said Lupe, who was visibly upset.

"It happened a few days ago," said Jenks, who looked at his father sitting in his wheelchair by the door.

The crowd was silent.

"Is he all right?" asked Ms. Waters.

"It's very serious," said Lupe, who was now in tears.

Ali was seemingly stoic, in shock over his grandfather's hospitalization.

"Would you like to wait to give your presentation?" asked Ms. Waters in her sweetest voice.

The three young friends looked at one another, not knowing what to say. Finally, Ali looked at Ms. Waters. "No, we will do our presentation. My grandfather would want us to," he said with conviction. Jenks smiled nervously, and Lupe dried her tears.

Ali, Lupe, and Jenks stood in front of their impressive display, their heads held high. The neat lettering at the top of the three-part display panel read, "Honeybees: Working Together for the Benefit of All Creatures." The crowd cheered wildly, especially Mr. Hooper. Lupe and Jenks smiled at each other and signaled to Ali that they should begin.

Lupe stepped front and center. "Imagine a world with no oranges, apples, peaches, raspberries, blackberries, cranberries, grapefruit, onions, cucumbers, avocados, cherries, blueberries, plums, cantaloupes, almonds, or honey. Breakfast, lunch, and dinner would not be the same. And what about not having pumpkins for Halloween? These are just some of the crops that depend on the honeybee. Honeybees are perfectly adapted for their environment and help all of us," she said, almost running out of breath at the end. She signaled to Jenks, who slowly took her place front and center.

He hesitated, finding it hard to start. He glanced at his father, who was blinking back tears and smiling with pride. Jenks looked to his two friends for support. Both smiled as he began. "*Apis mellifera*, the European honeybee. Beekeepers around the world have seen their colonies shrink in the past twenty years. In some places, up to seventy percent of the colonies died. This is called colony-collapse disorder. Scientists believe it is caused by many factors: mites, pesticides, monoculture, stress, and lack of genetic diversity." Jenks drew a deep breath and wiped the beads of perspiration from his forehead.

Ali smiled at Jenks and touched his shoulder as he took his place front and center.

Mr. Hooper looked all around at the other parents and, with tearful eyes and overwhelming pride, could not contain himself. "Jenks is my son, and those are his best friends," he said, smiling broadly.

There was a moment of uncomfortable silence, and Ali thought about his grandfather lying in the hospital.

"My grandfather was a beekeeper in Iraq. Because of colony-collapse disorder and the war, the bees and many beekeepers are gone. There is something special about honeybees. Honey is the only food that does not spoil. Sealed jars of honey have been found in Egyptian tombs over three thousand years old, and the honey is still edible. In his Nobel Prize speech, Dr. Martin Luther King Jr. said, 'We have inherited a big house, a great world house in which we have to live together—black and white, Easterners and Westerners, Gentiles and Jews, Catholics and Protestants, Moslem and Hindu, a family unduly separated in ideas, culture, and interests who, because we can never again live without each other, must learn, somehow, in this one big world, to live with each other,'" said Ali.

He choked up, and his friends joined hands with him. Ali took a moment to gather himself.

"Jady, my grandfather, taught me everything I know about honeybees. He taught me that honeybees, even though they are just a little thing compared to the problems of the world, are responsible for one-third of the food we eat. Bees work hard to pollinate our crops. And they have to fly nearly forty-eight thousand miles to collect enough nectar to produce one jar of honey. If bees can work that hard for us, we should work just as hard to save them," said Ali triumphantly.

The three friends all heaved a deep sigh of relief as they joined hands again. Ms. Waters applauded immediately. The crowd joined in and applauded wildly, led by Mr. Hooper, who was bursting with pride.

As the sun set after the science fair, the world had been made a better place as three young people were brought together through a shared mission for the greater good. Along the way, they had learned that cooperation, friendship, and compassion bound them together, and united they would remain, indivisible.

ABOUT THE AUTHOR

Bruce Olav Solheim was born on September 3, 1958, in Seattle, Washington, to hard-working Norwegian immigrant parents, Asbjørn and Olaug Solheim. Bruce was the first person in his family to go to college. He served for six years in the US Army as a jail guard and later as a helicopter pilot. He earned his PhD in history from Bowling Green State University in 1993.

Bruce is currently a distinguished professor of history at Citrus College in Glendora, California. He also served as a Fulbright professor in 2003 at the University of Tromsø in northern Norway.

Bruce founded the Veterans Program at Citrus College and cofounded, with Manuel Martinez and Ginger De Villa-Rose, the Boots to Books transition course—the first college course in the United States designed specifically for recently returned veterans. He has published five books and has written seven plays, two of which have been produced.

Bruce is married to Ginger, the girl of his dreams, who is a professional helicopter pilot and certified flight instructor. He has been blessed with four wonderful children: Bjørn, Byron, Caitlin, and Leif. He also has a precious grandson, Liam. Bruce, his brother, and his two nephews still own the family home in Åse, Norway, two hundred miles above the Arctic Circle.

ABOUT THE ARTIST

Gabby Untermayerova was born in Bratislava, Czechoslovakia (now Slovakia), in 1984 to Slovak-Hungarian parents. At the age of three, she left with her parents in what would be a three-year immigration adventure, eventually settling in West Covina, California.

Art has always been a therapy, an escape, and a way of addressing what cannot be put into words.

Gabby attended Citrus College while working at the Norton Simon Museum as a gallery attendant before attending the Laguna College of Art and Design in Laguna Beach, California. She graduated with a BFA in illustration.

She currently lives in the foothills of San Gabriel Valley and works as an artist and art teacher in Los Angeles and San Bernardino counties. Her free time is spent with her partner in crime, Anthony, and their young daughter, "Yaya."

CPSIA information can be obtained
at www.ICGtesting.com
Printed in the USA
LVHW062331270623
750974LV00002B/242

9 781544 013985